THEY CALL THE WIND MARIA

ALLIE DODGE

Table of Contents

I WISH that a single teardrop could be split apart and opened, read, and transcribed into words. It would say more than I ever could myself.

- Allie Dodge

DEDICATION

I dedicated this book to Chris, my husband, and Christian,
our beloved son.

Without their strength and survival skills, I would not be
here to write this.

FORWARD

I WISH THAT A DROP OF A TEAR COULD BE OPENED, read, and transcribed into words. It would say it all for me. by Allie

I HAVE NO IDEA how writers go about writing and creating a fiction novel. What great imaginations they must have in coordinating a theme scheme. The development of characters with complex personalities. Lucky me I get to use my real characters. I do not have enough of a vision to create words that will make one believe in them. I do not know where this story is going or how it is going to end. The only thing I do know is that I want you to be a part of it and help me along the way. I can only try to write a sentence on paper that I know is real — my perception of reality. What I'm writing about is probably easier to stay in focus, but on the downside, I cannot change either the beginning or the end. It will be as the universe plans. I'm just hoping that my memory serves me well, and its voice will stay sharp and real enough for you to believe in me. The most challenging part of writing this tragic event for you is that I have to relive it over many times to reveal the truth.   The process is DAMN painful.

In nonfiction you have to stay with the truth no matter how good or bad it is, or feels. In fiction you can get away with anything thing, you can say and do whatever you want. You are not accountable for your actions, in other words you can walk on water.

My thoughts are not clearheaded, so please bear with me and let us get through this together. Writing this story for you makes me feel that, sitting here in this dark, cold room (NO, I AM NOT ALONE). I am your window, I want you to look out and see what I see, feel what I am feeling, and please know that I don't mean to cause you pain. Suffice to say I cannot prove everything that I am writing about but none the less it is all true and if you hate it or it hurts you I am truly sorry. I am not sharing this because I'm a victim; I'm sharing it because I am a survivor. I want to give you the courage that you can make it through anything when you have faith in yourself.

NINE WEEKS PRIOR

I have NO TIME FOR A REHEARSAL!

Allow me to go back in time for a moment to visit the hurdles that lead us through these next few paragraphs. My nerve endings are still so bloody raw that I am suffering from "Post Dramatic Stress Disorder." Sadly, so is my whole family.

Barely three months before had we departed Ft. Pierce, Florida, on our 53-foot sailboat to Puerto Rico. It was a sailboat that had not proven itself seaworthy to us yet, partly due to delays with repairs, and bad weather. The law mandates that you leave the US waters if you are going to document your vessel or pay taxes to that state if you choose to stay. In our case, we live in the Caribbean.

On our first sea trial is waiting for the nerve-racking bridge to open, motoring around in tight circles and fighting an immense current. Then there is an unexpected tornado, sailing towards us and going in the same direction that we need to go. We decide that we will be moving faster than the tornado. Turning back was not a good option,

We still have other fifty-something bridges to go beneath. Most of the bridges leave us with barely a two-foot clearance. Hopefully, this will happen without incident during the shakedown, before heading first to the Dominican Republic.

Our crew of four consists of my hero Hubby Chris, the Capt of our boat, navigator, rigger, fix-it man. A bear of a man at 6.3, 200lbs, who has been fearless in his commercial diving jobs in which he raises or sinks ships for the government for the past 30 years. He sleeps in the cockpit with one eye open when not on his shift, but watching yours. He speaks three languages fluently and after a long stretch of sailing he might confuse you by speaking all three in one sentence.

Capt. Christian, with his hazel eyes, is a long haired brilliant flower child. He should have been born in the 60's, because he is an old soul beyond his years. He was born and raised on a sailboat at sea, and is a natural sailor. Christian did not want to make this trip period. He had made this trip before and it was a hellacious, tough one. Since the last trip has become a vegan and an herbal medicine man. It was called the "Thorn Passage" for a good reason. So much for sailing. However he did give into this one last trip to help out his much older parents.

Our highly intelligent, super talented inventor, 22-year-old crew member Eric E, always a smile on his happy, beautiful face, calls me mom. He maintains the engine and fuel issues. He is also an outstanding magician who entertained us while we are underway. He was able to apply what he studied to work the hard way. We very got lucky to have him on-board

I am a long-haired, green-eyed, very skinny gal. I am the cook, bottle washer, and can fill in most of the areas when someone needs a break or sleep. I was hubby's commercial dive partner for seven years until I became a mother, and that was the end of my diving career. I am Merchant Marine officer 100ton, Masters in Auxiliary & Sail, who doesn't want to be at the helm anymore. A thank God I am a retired Federal Housing Inspector. My passion is painting, writing stories, prose. I am a hungry reader, and I love to sing on stage. However, at this age, I enjoy many days of complete solitude.

Eric and Chris have to be in the engine room, every five hours or so resolving the issues every time the engine stalls, while I'm at the helm in this rolling hell. I am trying to hold back my nausea, albeit not from seasickness but fear and anxiety. After a full day of this situation, I peek my head into the engine room as a hot blast of air gushes out; it is an inferno down in there and simply ask Eric, "Why can't Christian go down into the engine? Eric has a kind of greenish-gray color on his soaking sweaty face, his arms covered with oil. "Can you teach Christian how to help you bleed the injector system?" I say, "Hold on, and wedge in well guys, please be careful and don't get burned." "Yes," Eric answers, but it will take longer than the last few, and it's risky down below. Christian response is, "Don't worry, Eric, I'll be the judge of my risks. Christian doesn't get seasick, but is sunburn red, soaked, and wearing more grease than the engine room, by the time they come back to the cockpit. I don't know how they can repeatedly stand the motion and heat—more stress.

To my relief, Chris takes over the helm, knowing that he is responsible for a boat that hasn't been proven 100% good under heavy seas, but the only way to know is to go through it.

I go down below to attempt at cooking something for these hungry men. Not going to happen. I need to be dexterous and withstand the swoons of movement while holding onto sliding pots and pans,

I think tonight's dinner will be sandwiches.

I do not pretend to be the captain of this ship. My hubby had received a false weather report from a passing ship and still hasn't forgiven himself even though it was not his fault.

IT WAS LIFE and death at times! A dire and dangerous situation. I was leaning into the cushions with my legs curled underneath, hands in my lap clenched tight as I stretched my neck to stick my head outside the plastic windows facing into the blasting wind and jetting rain just so the men couldn't glimpse my tears of hopelessness. At that moment, I prayed to the Heavenly Creator, to the Gods, to the Clouds, and to the Waves. I prayed in English and Spanish. "I Dios Mio Por Favor" These boys are too young to die, so I swore on my life that if our lives are spared that I will never ask anything from the Creators again. "You can do this! You have the power I say to them! I think I switched between five different religions in five hours.

The storm window was faster than predicted; our window for the weather, from Marathon and arriving in Manzanilla, was given by Noaa; was a five-day forecast. Unfortunately, the storm arrived one day early, which is plausible. An average forecast to follow would be valid for about three days. The breaking waves were 12 to 15 feet high, with winds gusting 35-45 knots. Believe me, if I say they looked and felt like 30 feet.

We are motor-sailing through the last part of the Old Bohemian Chanal, a 180-mile stretch. Wind and sea against us, which is between Great Inagua Bahamas towards CAP DU MOLE, NW of Haiti, where the engine stops. Its night time, no moon as we tack under sail to De La Gonave, which allows us to have a clement sea and to change filters again. Then after the filter change, we backtrack under power and seek refuge in Rade De Las Basse Terre, Isla Tortuga, for the rest of the night. We still maintained our watch shift. At first light, we depart motor-sailing heading 60-miles to Manzanillo, the first port of entry in the Dominican Republic. We spend a few days waiting for the right window (better weather) to complete our.

We endured this weather for a couple of days. We almost lost the boat and our family of four, but Due to the complete dedication, trust, and willpower of our team, we were victorious. There was only room for us and we in our dialogue.

TIME FOR THE MAIN EVENTS

The 2017 Season for Hurricanes has arrived, along with our first warnings for "Hurricane Irma" Our boat's name is "Espiritu Libre II" In English, it translates to "Free Spirit.

We have arrived in our home port Puerto Rico after surviving the freak; "Storm from Hell!" and hopefully, our home will survive another season.

Irma is on the way. We still needed to sail to Salinas, Puerto Rico, and we made it in a couple of days.

It took us two days of non-stop work, just the two of us to get the sailboat into the safety of the mangroves, girdled in tighter than a woman's corset. Add miles of two-inch line-rope cut in assorted 50ft (15.24 m) lengths. Then find the most durable mangrove tree trunks, tie them to the most prominent roots ten feet deep within. Clean up your cuts and bruises in which you get all over your body, while you are trying to squeeze into tight places.

Chris and I stayed on-board with a watchful eye to ride out Irma. It wasn't as scary as it may sound.

Mangroves are protected by law, so we remove

our sailboat out of them as soon as Irma passes.

We now have another mental and physical challenge. This task is also a demanding physical process, so we are moving slowly, dragging our feet. It almost makes us just want to stay tied up in them for the season if it wasn't for the laws and thirsty mosquitoes.

We are going to repeat this task for "Hurricane Maria." I remind you that we haven't had a recovery period, and only a week has passed since "Irma" was here.

Often, Chris turns pale and looks exhausted as he dizzily stumbles around the deck, looking as if he had been drinking in his haste to get everything ready. You do not imbibe during this period, the safety of your home and life depend on your sobriety.

A human only has so much will power and a limited amount of energy stored unless it has been stimulated or jump-started by adrenaline. We need rest and healing time to refill our mental and physical holding tanks.

In this case, mine is E for empty.

SORRY! No reserve tank left in this older 1954 model.

Meanwhile, "Hurricane Marina" is outside doing her best to arrive in full force. At this stage of the impending storm, she is supposed to have less wind and heading more south. But that doesn't happen.

Writing this is giving me a sense of security that "Yes! I did survive the "Dinghy-Trip-From-Hell": So, what's a hurricane when my feet are on solid ground.

I will write all day and every night, chasing after a piece of sanity, not to mention this is an excellent form of distraction. I am documenting this event in the dark, sitting on a very wet mattress. Droplets of water are dripping near my head. No sheets. I'm using a flashlight to see the keys of my tablet. I believe I will need more batteries. The rain, ocean, and muddy water are rising almost midway up the dresser drawers in my room. I am trying to figure out the new smells in my room. Oh no, I think it looks like seawater and sewer mixed. At this point, every increased inch: my pupils dilating, my eyes registering the depth, send little jolts to my brain receptors as in what are you going to do next, Allie? I can't get out of the room because three kayaks are blocking my door.

We'll get to that. Wait for it.

I don't want to forget this. Could I ever forget a life-changing event like this? Yes! And No! A mind has a way of adapting and consoling itself. Maybe even fooling itself in a desperate search for self-preservation. Sometimes I will just shut down as if nothing has happened and go on living a sail boaters dream.

In our early days, we did not always know where our next meal would come from, so we would scuba dive to catch dinner, lobster, and fish.

This, too, was in abundance years ago.

Living aboard a sailboat; working, sailing, and raising children, learning survival skills. You are always doing repairs, whatever it takes to keep her liveable and seaworthy, ask any sailor; it never ends.

We are travelers, and it is expensive, so your boat necessities become your primary occupation. We have adapted our jobs to be the sea-going ocean. The trick of survival is to learn how to do everything yourself. I learned over the years to repair my own sails, make dodgers and biminis, for other sailors. Yes, of course, it will take some time, but the lessons come about very quickly.

This is a choice of a risky lifestyle we made thirty-five years ago, we always knew there is a price for this freedom, and sometimes we just don›t wanna pay up.

We have spent most of our time in unknown waters, deserted islands, and between reefs: or job hunting. It was much safer solo sailing with your family years ago than it is today. That is the way of the Caribbean. We live to have new adventures and always try to be prepared and expect the unforeseen circumstances.

We have been on board, and in more than nine major named hurricanes, more than we care to remember. Even though we are very experienced, with plenty of how to do knowledge, experiencing many storms does NOT make them any less scary. I know for a fact that fears are almost always heightened, as your experience increases.

Chapter I

The storm update

I T'S almost midnight when Chris receives our last update for Maria, and the very latest phone communication any of us will have for weeks.

Our closest friends, Gabriel and his wife Wanda, on sailboat "Good Timing," call us. Gabriel announces, all in one breath. "Put your wet suits on, get your life jackets in your hands because "Maria" is a Furious Catagory 5 with winds of 155 mph, and is no longer heading north as anticipated, but has turned south towards you. You must make a decision now if you want to leave your boat and find shelter, period!

In reality, Gabriel tried to break the news to me first gently. I decide the tone of his voice indicates that he is holding something back, so I go and find Chris. This account is still a reasonably accurate description.

I don't know where this story is going or how it is going to end. The only thing I know is that I want you to be a part of it and help me along the way.

Chris hangs up the phone and gives me one of those looks. After over thirty-five years of marriage and being liveaboards, 24-7, it feels more like 50 years, I know exactly what the full piercing look in his dark eyes is saying to me, and the depth of its meaning.

Chris exclaims, "Maria isn't supposed to come this far south, and we are going to be in serious trouble, so we do not have enough time to go for plan B. What do you wanna take? Make some of your own decisions.

Chris calls our friends and fellow boaters, Rick and

his wife Sue, right away to ask him if it was possible to reserve a room for us at Marina de Salinas. Rick calls back within a few minutes and says, "Okay, Guys! You are good to go, and the only thing is you have to leave your boat right now! There is unquestionably no time for packing, so grab whatever is a must! There is only one room left, hurry up. We will see you when you get here!"

Pack up only what we need. Do I need underwear? Help!

I grab my 1500 thread count beige sheets, my personal favorites, off the bed only for speedy convenience, in which later I used to keep the water from coming under my door at the shelter.

Now in usual standards, we are considered an older couple. Let me inject a thought before I go too far. Living on boats is arduous work. No, we do not sit and drink margaritas all day. There are constant challenges in safety. There are always trials when sailing at sea: make yourself stay awake days at a time, thus gives you stamina. Even securely setting your anchor is a liability and a big responsibility for us and our fellow boaters. The daily challenges that we go through are what stand us apart from most people who live a more comfortable, secure, 9-5 life on land. We are in a constant body motion as the boat rocks. We become more energized than if we are sitting on a couch in a house. Just think we are burning calories while sitting, our bodies moving with the rhythm of the ocean.

Imagine doing your laundry, you have to get it into the dinghy, walk with it to the laundromat, get it back into the dinghy, and drive back to the boat. Just buying groceries too is an event, hauling the food back and forth by hand into the dinghy, then onto the ship before they perish. Most of us who are live aboard sailors and live on islands do not have cars. Don't forget your dog needs to go to land for his duties. Our awareness of the forces of nature, of the ever-changing ocean, has become enhanced and to be respected. We exercise daily by swimming or to keep our bodies cool. We find ourselves with more energy than most people that are our age. We have seen it time and time again.

Sorry, I am snickering, but it won't last long.

BACK TO the moment of packing

I FEEL A rush of panic but, and I am trying to push all thoughts out, trying to keep them at bay for a while. Okay! I am trying to think again. I can't pack

4

very well so then what do I bring? Rush! Hurry! Still, I cannot function six minutes later. Maybe I blocked my thoughts too well. It's hard to lift my feet, they are lagging. Nerves, I tell myself, calm down. I can hear Chris thinking out loud and repeatedly saying, "This sucks" in the background, which isn't helping me concentrate.

WE ARE SIX miles away from Marina de Salinas, the place that will be our shelter. Officials have evacuated all families in Salinas. We grab the briefcase which has been pre-packed, as always for this season and situation.

With the suitcase open, I shove in sheets, jeans, a few t-shirts, a few toiletries, a (stupid) smart phone, an iPad with GPS, a VHF radio that used to communicate from vessel to vessel. Most importantly, communicate with the Coast Guard on channel #16

We struggle into our tight black, warm scuba wet-suits. No food, no water. I looked at the box of granola bars on the counter. Yep! I'll grab these. "Any thing else?" I ask aloud: NADA! Nothing! Well, I did sneak a small bottle of Puerto Rican rum. I'm smiling, been there! At least I'll have some anesthesia for afterward.

In hindsight, I should have drunk half the bottle for what I will call‹ liquid courage› to get me through this night still to come.

We load up our two small suitcases into the dinghy, five flashlights, two headlamps, and jump in. Ready, we asked each other? Did we bring life jackets? Nah, now why would we need those? Considering we've been professional scuba divers for 20 years, we didn't bring a snorkel either. We still need to fill the main gasoline tank, grab an extra five-gallon container of fuel for our return trip. All of this is taking time, and we are running late.

AT THIS POINT I have no idea that we were going to ride all six miles in our little nine-foot dinghy, with its 15 hp Yamaha. Right now, this very minute after midnight, I think we are going to the Fisherman's Village, and we'll wing it from there. No way! In all the hurricanes, Chris has never abandoned the ship! He knows that I am not going to be able to cope well through this one if we stay on board, especially after what we have been through in the last two months at sea. He gave in to my plea, and we left the ship.

Chapter 2

Midnight Madness

66 Ready?" "Ready!"

We put on our headband flashlights and carried another in our hand.

Here we go blind as bats outta there trying not to run into and over the multitudes of boats and boat lines. We zigzag going under, around, over, and oops that one was close. That rope must have stretched at least two hundred feet across. Navigating this is very tedious and is taking too long to maneuver our way through to the exit. We do not know how many boats are tied inside the mangroves, as there are miles of them.

I do not start squawking until we go under the third tied-up boat, with lines that are attached everywhere into the mangroves. Around the tenth boat with spaghetti lines, I am sure Chris wants to throw me overboard if you get the big picture. I am repeating myself, mind you!

The GPS on our iPad is doing its job well, as we motor in a black moonless sky, through very long, narrow, and winding mangroves. The smell is strong, musky, and damp. I breathe in as if I have a surgical mask over my face. This trip takes about 40 minutes to find the open channel.

Destination heading west, is out in the wide-open channel. No! We didn't bring a compass. In twenty minutes, we will be sitting in the Marina bar, enjoying a pina-colada

The scenario looks like this, mangroves, rocks, and shoals on our right side. On our left side, there are tiny islands with reefs, some more shoals and rocks, and the open water. When you get somewhere in the middle, you cannot see either side in the pitch-black darkness. I mean, really! How far can a flashlight shine?

Once I'm aware of Chris's intentions, I start shaking in reality. I am retorting out loud to Chris. "We are not truly going to go this way, are we? Come on, get real, Chris! I am screaming into the air at him. "I can't do this... not going to do this... I can't do this!

If the motor dies, so do we! Turn around, please, please, Chris!" His face was devoid of any expression. He is deaf to my pleas. Chris simply says: "Please trust me, baby, one more time, I have never let you down." Honestly, I don't want to hear that right now, I just want to see the marina.

I try looking for lights in the blurry distance, and I keep blinking: the rain feels like tiny stinging needles because of our speed against the oncoming winds. Hmm. How can Chris see through this, I wonder? I empty the air from my lungs; I make a circle with my lips and pull in a breath only to find it is full of salt spray. I tell myself to concentrate on the GPS again. The focusing power of my mind is getting slower and very--- I think the word would be foggy.

The dinghy is filling up with water, and there isn't anything we can do about it. Too late, to turn around now. Wind speed is approximately 30 to 40 knots. The horrifyingly terrible realization, along with the dark foaming sea, is that we are going to die out here needlessly. After all, we have sacrificed and lived to tell. No way to say goodbye to the people we love; our mothers, our son, and our best friends. No one to call in this midnight madness plan of escape for survival.

The coastguard had already announced earlier that there would be NO emergency rescues during this Hurricane. It is simply impossible!

All I can think of is; we are out here with a loss of direction; fix the GPS. Every few minutes the sensor drops off the screen, it goes haywire, and the pre-hurricane winds are due to arrive shortly.

Meanwhile, I pull our clothes out of my suitcase and try to keep the iPad screen dry. Nylon T-shirt, nylon shorts nope they won't dry the screen, so I keep pulling assorted clothing till it feels like cotton, then feeling through for a new piece. Every ten minutes, I pick something else and keep going at it, while I am also afraid that this multitasking will make me drop the iPad at the bottom of the dinghy or, worse, overboard.

It is our only salvation. I am bouncing up and down. I try holding onto the handle with a grip that is hurting my hands and fingers. Not to mention, my hurting pancake buns.

Chapter 3

It burns, burns, burns

An hour later, the rain is non-stop, and it desensitizes the iPad screen. Our course is either zooming in and out or is just locked up. NOTE: I do not use the iPad- I use a computer.

Chris lets go of the steering handle to help me get the chart to straighten out while he is trying to center it. Not only are we getting rain but, the seas now are breaking over my shoulder. There goes our course again, and no way to tell which way is the right way.

The light from the iPad is so bright that all I can see are white dots in front of my eyes when I look away to find anything. There are tiny specks of light miles ahead in front of us and miles away behind us, and we have just spun in circles once again. Don't forget the shallows and the surrounding reefs.

We have been in this predicament for about two hours. I need to sit on the bottom of the dinghy because I just can't hold on anymore. The waves and winds are pushing me down, feeling frail I slide like a limp noodle. Maybe I should think of myself as a piece of seaweed. "Hey, Chris, do you smell gas fumes"?

Had this been day time, the trip would have been a smooth twenty minutes, without the need for a GPS.

A few minutes later, the waves are breaking over both sides. I'm yelling now: "Chris, I'm on fire!" I am trying to wedge my body parts; the gasoline tank has tilted over and is leaking. The dinghy is full of two inches of gas; I am trying to stop my whole body from slipping into the motor: My feet are slippery and covered in gasoline, and I can't get a place to wedge them. I remember my dive boots are in here somewhere: I guess I thought that I would have time to put them on. I sigh.

My visible tears of pain are just washing away with the salt spray. The dinghy has multiple garments floating around as I grab a couple and wrap it around my feet to gain stability, unable to hang on I slide around the bottom again. My body is now sitting half-covered with a mixture of saltwater and fuel. My long hair is stuck to me because the rubber bands keeping them in place have slipped due to the slickness. I have to mention that my delicate parts are on fire. It burns, burns, burns!

"Allie--Allee, try again with the GPS," Chris Yells. The iPad has now turned darker due to water seeping in between the screen protector and the glass. I frantically try to get the cover off of it, turning it at all angles. It seems to be like a Rubik's cube puzzle that takes some practice. My only answer is to start ripping it off. But I can't do it because the case seems made of a secret classified plastic material. Chris grabs it from me to get the edges peeled back. I declare. "Alright done!" Now, to find anything dry. Voila! The iPad springs to life again only to show me the complete chart of North America. Argh.

The water in the dinghy is so full and running out over the stern that it has triggered my imagination's negative side. I can't stop it. Multiple dread worthy scenarios assault me, mostly because I have been through many near-death escapes at sea in the past.

Filling up with anguish, along with the abrupt short waves that jar my neck and head back and forth.

I have images of fifteen-foot long limbs, whipping at us like ropes that will simply reach out and capsize us. Then throwing our little nothing of a boat, upside down into its hungry reef. Gnawing at our tender souls with vicious vapors tongues as hypothermia approaches.

Still imagining that we are holding on for hours. We are immersed underwater, over and over again. The only way to survive is to steal a breath of wet salty air. Hold on, hold on. Do I really want to go through this?

Chapter 4

Bail baby bail

Chris focuses on finding his direction. He gets invigorated by this kind of action and emotion. Me, well, I'm not feeling so confident.

I hear a strange sound that I don't recognize, only louder this time, calling out loud to Chris, "We are not going to make it through this one Chris, not this time."

I stutter I keep screaming into the air "I can't do this, not gonna do this!" It turns out that the horrifying sound is my voice. Chris looks intensely at me. He probably can't understand me anyway with all the noise. After a long silence, he says, "Trust me! I will never let you down." He leans over to me, grabs me by the arm tightly, and says, "Get a grip on your-self right now!"

Two minutes later, Chris yells, "Babe, start bailing the water out" "But, I don't have anything to bail with, "I replied. I mean, the dinghy is full! Full to one inch of the free-board.

I frantically grab one of Chris's floating T-shirts; spread it out in a scoop fashion with both hands spread wide, to use it for hmm, what? For the lack of an imagination? (I snicker) never leave home without a baler tied. Yep, you got it. It has floated overboard.

Chris has to yell to be heard over the engine and the winds. "Wedge yourself in, hold on tight baby." "I'm making a turn, and it might flip us! "Just F*cking great!" He says. "What? Can't hear you"? I answer. "It doesn't matter, does it?

We are now changing our course to empty the

water from the dinghy. The waves are getting even more significant. We are less than 150 feet or so, from the breaking reef ahead. A huge furling wave crashes over our heads and throws the dinghy up in the air; we do a 360 turn, and I can hear the propeller's cavitations' as it makes bubbles.

If the dinghy wasn't full of water, we would have been turned upside down permanently.

I can hear its roar, smell its foamy sweetness, I can feel the pressure of the buckets of cold water over my face that shock me!

Wind speed is around 40 to 50 knots. To top that off, it is going in a reverse direction, which we don't know at this time. The wind comes typically from the seaside, but it is coming from the direction of land. Other times it is blowing in a circular motion. We are airborne several times. This motion is so disorientating, leaving me dizzy.

I know the enemy is trying to keep me down, but I can't see it yet. My Eyes are wide, leery, scouting, and protective. There is no holding on for me anymore, and I have no strength in my hands against the forward speed, which throws you backward. The spare gasoline tank has turned over completely.

There are three feet of liquid at the bottom of the dinghy as I sit in it, staying there, whether I want to or not.

Chest-deep, still burning.

TWO and a half hours later, a coppery taste evolves in my mouth. My tongue is swollen and stuck to the top. I recognized it as the taste of fear, copper that has become a symptom over many years. We fear the unknown. My anxiety is tearing a hole in the realities of hope.

Another jagged lightning bolt has split into many directions looking for a place to ground itself. I swear that I think it's looking for me? Fear is making me nauseous. I want to throw up so bad! I would enjoy getting that out of my system — no such luck.

"Now, where the f*ck are we?" Chris says out loud to himself. "This is very comforting!" I say under my breath. With numb fingers, I start throwing the shorts, T-shirts out of the boat, along with sticks, mangrove branches, mangrove leaves. Whatever touches my fingers at that moment is thrown overboard.

Chris shouts. "What the hell are you doing?" I don't speak. I just think who gives a DAMN right now. I can't even get the drain hole cleared.

"Bail, Baby, Bail!"

We are trying to move at top engine speed so that the waves behind us don't catch up, and we can drain the water out, and of course, we are off the path again, as we become airborne once more. The first bands of heavy wind and rain are pouring on.

We both sit silently for a long time, running downhill, draining it out.

Chris breaks the silence by saying softly yet still loudly, "I love you!"

I don't answer, staying silent. Helplessly I cannot speak. My subconscious is speaking to me again. Implying things like "Let's see, that would be winds of 155 mph, enduring 12 hours plus, not including the pre-winds. No rescue possible even if they did know our approximate position.

Out of nowhere in fear! "NO, NO!" with a blood curdling scream to the wind. I curse the ocean, the sky, shouting more potent than the roar of wind and seas. "I can't take this Chris, "I don want-wanna-try, don-don't wanna survive in this nightmare."

I don't have any fight left in me. Chris gets a shake-up call. I say! Really! "Please call 911, call the Coastguard." Chris registers, and said, "It won't do us any good! They won't be able to find us, and our signal isn't any good." "Can we try at least please, please" I'm begging. My tone indicates my level of hysteria.

I promise myself right now that if any of these fears that I am hosting become a reality, any one of them happens, that right this minute, "Forgive me Mother of the Universe and its Creator." I will gladly, painlessly, slide over the side, and breathe in deeply as I can and promptly be done with it, swallowed by the sea, a pain-free sleep. I wouldn't call it a suicide.

Looking into the depths of the waves reaching my side and feeling the warmth in my wet-suit sends me down memory lane. I remember my mother would fill up the bathtub to the very top with hot water and bubbles.

I would put one foot in at a time to test the temperature, and then slowly, insert my toes and wait-feet-wait-knees. A custom to the heat I would take a deep breath, hold it and close my eyes dunk my head under the water and lay there enjoying the quietness, the darkness, and solitude of absolute silence. I would repeatedly do this until the water was lukewarm, soap up, and wish it was hot again. How I long for this right now, it will only take me two minutes to be there. Jump Allie!

Chapter 5

We see the light

I don't remember ever being so afraid, or desperate in my all my sixty-three years, that I would prefer death. In seas, on a 53ft (16.15 m) sailboat, even in 20-foot seas, we stand a chance of surviving. I would be selfless for the life of our beloved son and Eric. I would have a life jacket, and I would be hanging on to boat parts and holding them close to me. Chris already knows my wishes if he had to make that choice between them or me.

ONCE AGAIN I try to get air into my lungs, only to be assaulted by gallons of saltwater. I start coughing like the seas slamming against the rocks. It fills my nostrils and is sticky in my hair. "I swear this moment is more than I can bear."

Another bolt of lightning lights up the whole sky, leaving a memorized streak of our visual direction.

Chris shows me his teeth; I am guessing that's a smile. Feeling confident, he is steering towards the correct mangrove point because there are tiny lights in the shadows that he can recognize the mangroves' silhouette near the next entrance. I try so hard to distinguish the mangroves which resemble film negatives — looking for lights in the blurry, deep distance. I am still blinking out the tiny stinging needles of rain in my already droopy, drenched eye sockets.

Right about now, I am calming down. Why? I want to feel the nothingness. I sigh, resigned! I am just a limp form lying in the pool of burning liquid. Gratefully my mind is underactive. I don't even remember my moral code of life "TO NEVER GIVE UP." I do associate surviving our last storm with our family months ago, and I promised the Universe that I would never again ask for salvation. I want to pray, and I need to pray. I need to believe in God and the Universe to help us and guide us to the illuminated path. I want to take that promise back—no prayers to be made this time, no pleading for mercy. But I can still have faith and hope!

I have no idea what Chris looks like or is doing, besides sitting on the rubber pontoon side of the dinghy holding the engine arm in one hand, and the other on the grip, But I know he must be in some pain as well.

He looks intensely at me with concern in his eyes and gives me an empathetic smile. He seems to see me for the first time.

After what seems like hours upon hours: just try to convince me otherwise. After all, it is how I see things. (I smirk again)

The lightning lit up the black sky so bright that I might have called it a spectacular light show in another time and place.

Chris can see the contrast between the sparkling sea and the mangroves' line. The correct direction to take is vivid. Theoretically, the other indicator is the reversed wind. We now have a look for a calmer sea surface, which will indicate the closeness of the seashore.

Chris says that he has found his bearing. I call it his inner compass.

I snap out of my limp body with a jolt of excitement.

I pee in my wet-suit. The warmth is saturating and satisfying, which considerably helps my delicate burning situation. I wondered what took me so long!

I sit up on top of the dinghy pontoon, craning my neck to see better, I am desperately searching for the sign of hope Chris has promised me.

I yell, "Go port, go to port! Oops!" Not yet, that one has a reef in front of it. Whew, that's a close one."

I suck in and breathe deeply for the first time as I blow through my puckered lips, a sigh of relief. We move fifty yards farther west. Chris makes his decision for a final turn in the dark. "Starboard, starboard," YEAH! We say together.

We would have jumped up and down if our bodies had permitted this. Now I see what looks like an enormous tree immediately in front of us as loudly I say, "port go, f*cking port! I can talk this way; I am a sailor-girl after all... Hee hee! The enormous tree turns out to be the stern of a very welcomed, large powerboat that we barely avoid hitting. Regrettably,

I think it was adrift.

We have finally arrived at our entrance with a long way to go., and we are making a tediously slow track through the drifting boats. Boats are anchored and strapped in again with fettuccine lines everywhere, sorrowfully many of them have drifted early on in the pre-storm winds and will not make it back. They will either sink or get thrown up into the mangroves. In the worst-case scenario, they could potentially drag and sink additional boats along the way that had anchored in the various areas.

Chris stretches over and squeezing my leg, Says, "See baby" with a big, gentle smile of a hero. "I told you to trust me! My guardians never let me down."

I'm thinking, will I drown him now or later for putting me through this?

(My turn to smile)

No, wait! I'm not on land yet. He truly is my hero! I am not going to give him the gratification of forgiveness right now.

Chapter 6

The shelter

We arrive at Marina de Salinas around 2:30 am. Weather Report says;

Maria will be at its full force between 8:30 am and noon.

I can barely feel my rubbery, numbed legs. I drag myself up and onto the pier with my numb hands that are burned and withered. I crawl on all fours about five feet to test my legs and finally stagger drunkenly up onto two. Drunk? Not yet!

I have no recollection of what Chris was doing right then. Probably getting our drenched things onto the pier, or looking for a location to secure our dinghy.

I see the shape of a familiar frame heading towards me. "I squawk with a cackling voice. OH, My God! It's Rick!" I have never been so delighted to see him as in right now.

He gives me a big welcome squeeze, and an indispensable arm to hold onto because my feet are not obeying the brain signals. "But-butt--how did.--dd you know that we were here?" I ask. Well, it turns out that they knew; what I did not know! We would be coming via dinghy through the channel.

Sue has been keeping a lookout for us from the hotel shelter room window on the second story.

On the way to our room on the first floor, I am laughing at myself while trying to get my left leg to cooperate, which thinks I have left it in the dinghy; to cross over loose boards, coconut shells, floating garbage, endless debris. This is part of the aftershock reaction.

Somehow, I find myself standing alone on the second floor with a group of strangers. All of them have drinks in their hands, conversing loudly amongst the group. They seemed very intense about whatever they were saying. All of a sudden, it gets quiet. I look around at the gathering. What just happened? You got it, I just happened!!

In unison, they all turn their heads to see the new arrival. Really! I look like something you only see in the movies. I want to just crawl under the stairs, and run away, but to where precisely?

I am hugging my skinny self with both arms around my slimy black wet-suit, reeking of gasoline. My two-foot-long straight, wet sea-weeded hair, now looking like unkempt dreads, the very envy of Medusa. My eyes with red veins are bulging, drooping, bewildered, and full of fear. Horror! Of what? Unknown to me, my old waterproof mascara is smudged under my eyes, presenting me an even more of a dramatic look. Come on, anyone would laugh at that!

Everybody could see that something tragic has just happened to this lady, so they avoid any form of eye contact. Not that I can blame them! One woman chances to make eye contact with me; she makes eye contact again and can see past my exterior appearance. Yes! Relief flushes over my body like a burst of warm rays. She is making a move towards me, eyes twinkling. Says in one sentence, "OMG You poor thing! What on earth has happened to you? Never mind, let us take care of you. Do you know what you need? Who are you with, are you alone?" "Hi!" she hesitates.

"I'm Shelly, she says, with a proper English accent. Shelly wraps her arms around me for the encouragement that I needed right this minute. I try to talk but not even comprehending where to begin.

I'm not making enough sense. Appreciatively, Shelly is doing the talking for both of us. All I can do is try to give her a quivering, encouraging smile.

Chapter 7

The first room

I finally get to our designated place on the bottom floor. Who delivered me here? I haven't the faintest clue. The first thing I do is to remove my soaking wet, salty, gasoline wet-suit, and jump into a hot shower. Most people said: There was no hot water. It is hot! Hot to me. (Big smiles here.)

Uh! Okay, so now I'm rinsed but only have my wet clothes to put on. What to do? Is this an issue?

Nope, not really! All of our garments are soggy with salt water, and I'm becoming cold again. I throw on Chris's wet, large T-shirt and hold my head out the door.

I still don't know where Chris is or what he is arranging; frankly, I don't give a Dam! I am just gonna be self-centered, and slowly try to piece myself back together.

Outside there is a lot of activity; boisterous, with people shouting over the groaning and growing winds. Many are just out walking around, some are kind of dazed while the others letting curiosity get the best of them.

There is an attractive, full-figured woman who is also standing in her doorway looking out at the developing storm; while tracking her husband. I shyly describe, in Spanish, my circumstances and beg for a dry shirt of any kind. Honestly and fairly, she isn't thrilled with the idea at first, considering she has only brought minimal clothing. I wave a twenty-dollar bill at her for something to wear. She is openly looking me up and down, trying to figure out what this skinny soaking wet lady can fit into of hers.

She searches through her possessions as I ask

her name. "Maribel," she responds. "Why are you so skinny? She asked me. She is handing me a very sexy beige top that looked like a spaghetti-strapped disco top. I was a little embarrassed about wearing this, so I threw on my wet, salty bra underneath, "ugh" pulled it over my head, and stepped out again to appreciatively thank her while handing her a twenty. She just looked at the twenty and said she didn't want it. I told her that I am not on a diet, and when we have some time, I'll explain my story about why I am so thin. Maribel rewards me with a pair of sexy, gray stretchy pants that will surely do the trick. I return to my room, take off the braided rope from the suitcase handle, and tie the pants on.

For the next three days, I am still wearing the same clothes. Maribel and I are hugging and joking about it as I share my long sailing story with her. I promise Maribel to return her clothes when this was all over. I carefully washed and dried them, but never saw her again at the marina. Can I have that shot of rum now? Thank you very much! Make that a double!

The hotel rooms in the marina area are in a horseshoe configuration, with a couple of pleasant statues, huge planted pots, and attractive decorations.

There are rows of kayaks, tied and stored in stacks of three and four in the center. I am in a room with double beds on the first floor of the two-story building. Over one of the beds, the ceiling is leaking a steady drip of rain on top of it. The bed I prefer is mostly dry. I have succeeded in sleeping for five hours, perhaps I should say passed out?

It's quite early in the morning as I reach for my tablet.

I think of you, Did you miss me?

Hurricane Maria is arriving and is expected to be 180 knots. The winds and seas are picking up and are flooding the hotel shelter's parking lots. The palm trees are leaning at a 45-degree angle, their coconuts are dropping like small bombs and palms flying high. Anything that is not, or cannot be tied down is becoming airborne or floating with the incoming current.

I hear sounds and voices approaching from the others that are stirring about. I've been awake for hours already typing incessantly. I massage my sore hands together. Stretch my arms and legs from the uncomfortable position and venture outside. I need to find a bottle of water and a snack. I'll eat anything at this point. Uh! Just don't offer me canned sardines, please.

Still emotionally out of it and do not know the etiquette for "How to ask for food and water?" Especially from other homeless people who brought only their minimal food and water supply to the shelter. There were many people seeking shelter at the marina. If not for their support and hospitality, many people would be homeless and desperately hungry. Number one would be me. Guess I'll eat a couple of granola bars. I would rather starve than talk to someone right now.

I am back in my room, where the water level has now reached a much higher level, almost up to the first drawer of the antique white wicker dresser. I am watching the water rise, counting the minutes until Chris will come back to check on me. I look out the front jalousie windows, but I cannot see what it looks like out there. Wow, I could not get out of those if I had to. I crack the door to go out, take a look around, and water pours in, flooding the room even higher. I think about the situations and wonder if I have any cuts on my feet or legs. OMG, I have cuts on the side of my foot that I got getting out of the dinghy with the obstacle course. I grab the rum bottle and pour it straight over the open cuts. Well, it is alcohol, isn't it?

The kayaks have made a 180-degree turn-around and are now obstructing the front of my door, keeping me from closing it. I shove them, huff and puff a few minutes and try again with all I possess in my little ninety-seven pounds frame. After a big struggle, I finally triumph!

It is time for me to make some kind of move without Chris. I throw the two suitcases we brought on top of the dresser, climb back on the bed to continue writing the events.

I desperately need something else to distract me from my exhaustion and negative thoughts. "I HAVE TO SAY THIS NOW TO YOU MY READERS THAT I AM A VERY HAPPY, POSITIVE, ENERGETIC, CAN'T WAIT TO SEE WHAT TOMORROW BRINGS, TYPE OF PERSON IN MY DAILY LIFE!"

I am thinking. Now, what am I going to do? I hope Chris comes back soon because I can't get out of the room in this situation. I am standing up and jumping on the bed for practice, and it seems okay. "I can do this!" I say, out loud to my cold, wet, prison room.

Maybe two hours have passed. The water level is up to the middle drawer. I cannot remember the time-lapse anymore, I just don't know! What I do know is that the water is now up in the third drawer. "OMG, haven't I had enough yet?" Furniture is beginning to float around the room. Wicker chairs paddled into the hall, and the cushions went next, following it like fluffy ducklings following their mother.

BREAK

I worked as a housing inspector during six major "hurricane disasters under a subcontractor for FEMA, and I know what can happen, like uh, six to eight feet of flooding inside and muddy. I cannot even begin to describe where my thoughts are right now. You wouldn't wanna hear it.

No problems, open the door, wait till the water reaches its maximum, and swim out. Only the brave and in the movies. Ha ha, No!, I won't hide from the kayaks in the bathroom either.

I hear a racket at the door as I yell to be heard at Chris to be careful when he opens the door. Of course, you can see this one coming. The water arrives barreling in with him. "Alright, let's get the f*ck outta here!" Chris says. "It's about time, did you forget me?" I ask. "Can't explain it all right now let's go, go, Chris says sternly.

So up we go to the second floor hauling our bags, suitcases, wet-suits that are still gas-wet, along with us. To our relief, we have volunteers in a few rooms who will share their space. The first room is full of people sharing double beds. I am bodily dragged in and sat down on a bed. Shawn, bless him, who turns out to be Shelly's husband, makes me a fantastic cup of coffee. Believe it or not, it made me wanna cry. The attention he put into preparing for a woman he doesn't even know, but it looks like she could use more than just coffee.

His wife, Shelly, wraps her arms around me and says, "It will be all right; just relax in here with us a while" I look at the smiling faces in an already crowded, peaceful room, knowing it would be imposing for me to stay. I remember chatting with a few people, but I am quite sure I made little sense. I don't recognize Shelly, my heroine, from the night before. Due to confusion on my part, Shelly takes over again and is very supportive of me.

Chapter 8

Room II

The next volunteers are two veteran sailor guys, who have their boats, out in the storm as well. They are sharing a room with double beds. "Sure, you can move in with us, but one of the beds has a leak over it," says Jean. "No problem! We will take your kind offer," I say.

Chris drops all the baggage, myself included, and disappears again. Taking a second look at me, they determined that I need to lie down next to Jean on his dry bed. (I'll take that too) "I bet you are hungry!" Andy says, I just roll my eyes at him, being still slow to speak, as he proceeds to make me a thick ham and cheese sandwich. I haven't eaten anything other than granola bars since 6:00 pm the previous day.

Chapter 9

They Call The Wind Maria

The guys keep us busy by sharing engaging real-life stories and taking turns mopping the water out through the open door. It is continuously soaked from the roof and leaking to the floor.

As our days go on, we have become good friends, always searching for each other for comfort, entertainment, and knowledgeable conversation. Our standing joke is that we are sleeping together...

It gets funnier each time we hear it, and it makes us laugh as the version seems to change according to whom we tell it to, including Chris. Jean, with his humor, protecting my reputation, says, "She is safe; I can only talk about it at my age."

The girls working and helping with literally everything around the marina, whom I don't know yet, hear about our little dinghy expedition and our emergency escape and feel sorry for me. They move us to a private, double bedroom that is also dry. The guys invited themselves to move in. "SORRY! I say, I'm sweet, alright, but not sugar."

I need to be alone with my healing, traumatic thoughts and continue writing these events. Maybe even a little time, for a pity party.

Chris enters our new room aggressively, grins, and gives me a detailed report. He assures me that he's going on a crusade against Maria.

"Please don't go. Don't leave me, please! I beg. Chris replies, "Don't you know me by now?" His warm golden-brown eyes that I fell in love with were shining at me. He walks over and plants a very delicate kiss on my pursed lips. "Please be careful!" I say softly.

I told you my smirks won't last.

The dinghies are tied up and secure, and we know how to do it without knowing how high the incoming surge will be.

Chris goes out an hour later to check ours, only to find that most of the dinghies are getting squashed against the concrete walls, and their motors are getting bashed. So, a team of men staying here joins Chris during the storms almost worst! They are struggling with the gusts of wind, ducking the huge flying aluminum sheets, nearly missing them as the group glides the dinghies through the current and tuck them into protected corners. They insist that it was a calculated risk and that they were watching all of the flying objects and timing them. They had to open a remote electric gate that was on a track to move the cars that were filling up with water. The water level at the electrical box is two feet high, bubbling, sparking, and smoking. Chris cuts the chain; eventually, the water absorbed the electricity and killed it.

Standing on my tiptoes, I can feel my chest, a slight thumping as I watch them through the bathroom window.

They ducked behind the fence from the flying objects and timed the gusts to make a move. Then they were able to push some of the cars through and float out the dinghies to a securer location.

The dinghy is our only means of transportation and also very expensive to replace. What about their lives?

I rush to my tablet and update these events, as I realize that I am holding my breath.

Breathe __Allie Damn it!

I spend the entire time, either writing or behind my camera filming or hugging close to the concrete walls with groups of people that I have come to know and have grown feelings towards them. They are doing the same and having similar stressful expressions on their faces.

Many wives are just like me trying to get a glimpse of their husbands.

We altogether are watching Hurricane Maria's incredible intensity of nature's destruction in the process. It lifts the roofs and shingles one by one off of the houses, and tosses them in the air like paper planes. Trailer homes that I can see from the rear balcony are being peeled like bananas, making a screeching metal sound that belongs in a horror flick, just up and disappears before our very squinted eyes.

Trees are pushed, plucked, blown over, and uprooted like stalks of celery. The powers lines are snapping loose, seeking out, and zapping around like snakes striking their targets. They are making me very jumpy.

The sound of the glass windows breaking or cracking as they fall, or explode from suction as the wind goes in one side of the house and comes out the other.

Scary noises surround me, leaving most of us with tattered nerves.

I join Jean on the balcony to share his agony; I put my arm around his shoulder as we watched his beautiful sailboat being battered, and finally sink.

Right now, as I am following cars floating down the streets in all directions, looking like they were on a conveyor belt, with refrigerators, coolers, TV's, strangely chasing after them. I wondered which person's front yard they will all end up in. Sadly, I see a couple of animals struggling, joining the current. I hope they make it through this.

Chris, being a tough guy that he is, did not think twice before running down to save a dove hiding inside of a brick of all things. I found myself pleasantly surprised to see his soft side on display. But then I think to myself, what am I going to do with a dove? Indeed a bittersweet moment.

We also saved a litter of wee and fluffy frightened kittens and then reunited them with their anxious mother. As the hurricane passes over a couple of days and with the sea conditions have improved, Chris breaks it to me that he has to leave to go check on our boat.

He thinks that I would be better off in the shelter's safety until he has surveyed and gotten hold of the situation back at home, but he leaves that choice for me to make. As I am still shaken up, I decide to remain in my room writing. I helped him drag the dinghy back to the ocean. He brushes his hand against my cheek and gives me a gentle kiss, but in the next moment, I hear the engine start, and Chris is gone. He knows that I will find my way back to him when the time comes, as I have in the past.

This reminds me of the time when we were living on our sailboat in San Juan during Hurricane Hugo 1989. Hubby Chris was out rescuing boats during

Hugo. Our first sailboat was thrown up into the Parque Central during that Hurricane. We made several newspaper headlines at the time.

I will make some notes so you can look up the articles.

(Boat dwellers terrorized by looters)

Our son was conceived during the Eye of Hurricane Hugo; therefore, he was named Christian Hugo and ironically was born on the first day of Hurricane season on June 1. Our joke is No TV.

Did I mention that I escaped the lockdown shelter through the bathroom window to go in search of my husband during that storm?

SLEEP IS evasive! I'm counting sheep backward. 99, 98, 97...

Chapter 10

Return to the boats

I t's high time I start trying to find a way back to the boat. I walk carefully on the now broken staircase, leading to the top of the roofless restaurant. It would probably be safer to climb a coconut tree. I try to get a signal and use the VHF radio. It was very emotional the first time I make contact with Chris and hear his voice since he left me more than three long days ago.

His voice sounds shaky. Chris says: "When you think you can handle it baby come home. If you want more time on land, take it." We lost our VHF signal after that sentence. That's a no brainer. I need to be with Chris to make sure he doesn't overdo himself. Chris is prone to work until he drops or takes on a task that requires two to three men. I swear he is from another planter. I am anxious to find out about the damage and how our home has survived.

Shawn finds me and enthusiastically asks, "Do you want to go with us in the dinghy back to the boats"? The small group in the dinghy, all eyes on me this time, doesn't faze me. "You must be kidding!" I said as I break out laughing uncontrollably. Shawn says to them, "Is she alright?"

I spread the news to groups that I will gladly pay a handsome amount to anyone who gives me a ride to the pier. No dinghy rides, please!

Most of the cars returning to the marina have flat tires and are left out on the road. The vehicles that stayed were flooded are either in need of serious repairs or beyond rescuing. A few were on a high enough ground; they only got wet carpets. There are so many obstacles that no one wants to be out there taking the risk, not to mention live power lines lying on the ground.

I finally get notified by a young couple that they will take me to the pier. Michelle and Antonio, but first, they must change the flat tire that they got after delivering the last person to their house. It is not just the car trip but also the fact that there are no gasoline stations to fill the tank. Gasoline is worth gold during this time. No water for your radiator, no tire shop to fix your flats. NADA!

I tidy up the room and pack as many of our things as I can. Then, I run down to the ocean side to fill a bucket of water and flush my toilet for the last time.

Hours later, I am on my way to my boat-home; we have to go over or by some live electrical wires on the road. In other areas, there still is three feet of water we have to find our way around. I was impressed with Antonio's driving decisions and swift responses.

I can't believe what my eyes see. Do I want to write about what I see **out** here?. I think writing this part now will only add to my distress. Yours' as well.

Even though I seem to feel emotionally more stable today, what I see is just too painful. So, for now, I will say only one word — "Catastrophic" all the areas that we cross.

Michelle and I are having a fun moment playing catch with a 20 dollar bill, from the back seat to the front seat and to the back again. "Please keep it; you took a big risk to drive all this way and bring me here." "NO!" she repeated. Finally, I shove the money in the ashtray and quickly get out.

I know we will meet up again at the marina.

Chris is expecting me at a pier that is broken in many places. It is only a 15-minute dinghy ride back to the boat, and I am all smiles. Chris looks like he has been dragged through the mill. We are both teary-eyed and hug and smooch a lot.

Chris maneuvers the dinghy with caution due to a bunch of floating objects in the canal.

I say: Wow--omg! What a sight! To see the boat in such a beat-up condition, but she is in one piece. Until now, I hadn't received any information other than we still have our home. It looks like a train wreck inside. I can tell it has been in a rodeo. She always wins a blue ribbon in my book. Yes, I am now grateful that I wasn't on board during Maria.

She had been thrown around so severely, scars and wounds remain.

The boat is sitting-stuck perpendicular to the canal.

I'm not going into every little detail just yet, because we feel very fortunate to still have our home. The majority of boaters and homeowners are in despair, just like us. It will take some dollars and six months to a year of repairs to make her home again. This isn't our first rodeo, either.

This time I pray with thankfulness. We clean the mud, seaweed. Look for our missing items in the trees. Try to make sense of the wash-a-machine mess that we have.

Make the necessary repairs, straighten up as much as possible, and make it livable. Get it ready once more to make a voyage. We have decided to wait until the hurricane season is entirely over before returning home port.

I wish we had left because a few weeks into the aftermath of the hurricane, I get bit by a mosquito that is carrying Chikungunya. I become so sick that I have become delirious, vomiting so violently and frequently that dehydration has set in. My heaving stomach is now dry and empty. A rash has grown on top of my stomach. This looks and feels like an ant farm has set up a camp. My legs keep jumping on the bed involuntarily like they are being sprung by bungee cords out of my control. I try to sit up, and I just hurt so much and ache all over that I flop back down again. I say to myself...Allie, you know...--you have been through worse.

Oh, how I love my feather pillow and closed-cell foam bed padding.

I don't know how long the fever lasted; neither does the hubby. All he knows is (do not give the person aspirin.) Give her plenty of rest and liquids.

Hey, I'm the Doc on-board. I think I should write a chapter for the hubbies, don't you?

There are no doctors available at the moment; they also have just gone through a hurricane that has also brought the mosquito fever with it and rumbling disasters to their homes and families. No exceptions.

The hospital has no land power and is using the back-up power generators. We did find a mom-and-pop pharmacy that gave me some medicine.

I can't tell you the name because they were just taking care of me with no doctors to prescribe medications. I call them the "mercy pharmacy." You'd have to kill me to get me to tell you. Ha-ha, All I know is that the walls of my cabin have been closing in on me one at a time. I have been bedridden for almost another two weeks.

I feel the need desperately to go upstairs, so I climb the five steep stairs, which feels like a mountain to me, onto the deck. Yes, some fresh air! It is a bright and beautifully sunny day, with a slight breeze.

I can almost feel healing in the process. I lay on the cushions for as long as my aching body can endure it. Chris plays my favorite tunes on the iPod and brings me some ramen noodles with an egg dropped in.

Not realizing how weak my petite limbs are, and I'm slightly dizzy on my way back down the staircase, my eyes haven't adjusted to the change of lighting down below.

I reach for the railing and miss, but my left-hand gets stuck in the handle. I release, stumble, and tumble down, kind of bouncing, head over heels, hitting my head on the built-in icemaker on the other side of the floor.

Chris is working on our water tank supply and repeatedly made sure that I was aware. I know I have a concussion because I have blacked out for about a minute. I am not sure as to how this exactly happened. I open my eyes, and I am lying here, stunned as to WTF has happened. In a matter of days, I am calculating my injuries.

I have fractured two ribs, fractured my left hand, broke my pinkie, sprained my ankle (don't know how), and my head has lumps the size of dried plums. I'm going back to hibernate in the safety of my cabin. Ice packs, ibuprofen, and I are going to have another pity party! Maybe, another week has passed, and I am feeling very stubborn, but optimistic.

I am so determined to get out of this bed that I recollect my yoga days coming to the rescue. I will just take baby steps in my daily life.

Physically I started to come around, but all of a sudden, two months later, I'm losing my speech patterns.

I find that it's tough to concentrate or to speak full sentences. Everything Chris asks of me is a big f*cking deal to answer and he cannot come to terms with what's happening to me either. He is upset and short of patience with my replies. I also am situated in a self-analyzing process, looking for some answers.

I am stuttering, slurring slightly, and the realization is a real stinger. I am explaining to Chris that obviously, something has short-circuited in my brain or memory functions. I realize that I have no control over this. I have a blank look in my eyes, but behind them, I genuinely am thinking. Is this permanent; temporally impaired? Fight! Allie fight! Just can't get the words out.

This must be what my mother, an Alzheimer patient, felt like when she knew that she was losing the battle.

Haven't I been through enough!! Before you get mad at Chris, he finally gets it. He takes significant action! He asks questions in a few different arrangements, even switching from English to Spanish or French because we speak all three: until he gets through to me. Chris helps me put on my clothes, brush my hair, gives me lots of water. Most important is that he says to me, "You are going to be alright. Remember what you are made of, my Babe."

Chapter 11

Recovery

Chris goes to town with Wanda and Gabriel. Their sailboat "Good Timing" was unbelievably spared, but they still went through an enormous struggle. They have driven their car for four hours to help us load up on dinghy and generator fuel; for both their own boat and ours as well. No rental cars, no taxi. Nada!

You probably will not believe this, but in the beginning, Wanda waited from 5:30 am in a gasoline station line for ten hours just to buy some gasoline and diesel for both of our boats weeks after Maria. We are on rations of five gallons per person. We also have a strict curfew that NO ONE is allowed on the streets before 6:00 am and not after 6:00 pm. Disobey and you get yourself a ticket and not a one to Disneyland!

Wanda told me that she would hide behind the bank at 5:00 am, after having left her house in Caguas at 3:00 am. She would wait till the curfew lifted at 6:00 am and then rush around the corner to join the line of the other 35 cars with their engines running, waiting to rush the front line as well.

Wanda repeatedly sat in the car with boiling summer heat, almost cooking herself with no air conditioning. It was hell if you opened a window due to fumes of the other vehicles whose owners are too afraid to shut down their engines. So, she too is sitting in fumes and waiting hours, many times over the days. Her windshield reflection cover was also no help.

When she got to our boats with her first twenty gallons, she looked like a pickled beet, pink all over. I asked, "Wanda, what has happened to you?"

She explained that she is severely toasted from

the sun's reflection through the windshield. The temperature inside the car would be 105 F.

Our group has spent hours in a line that stretches over two blocks, just to enter into the Amigos' grocery store. You have to wait! Only ten people are allowed in at a time. Chris gets priority to go in being a senior. You wouldn't believe the riot if a person tries to cut the line. I'm not going to mention that Wanda and Gabriel have a house with a family to take care of as well.

They take Chris to load up his grocery cart up with every munchies, fruit, and veggies that he thinks I might be able to eat.

Eat, baby, eat!

"This, too, Shall Pass Saith the Lord."

I have not been writing for quite some time now. Do I know how long?

Nope! Many months I can only assume.

Two more months or so have passed, and all I care about is trying to complete a sentence and maybe understanding what people are trying to say or ask of me. I prefer to visit only with close family and friends. I have enough psychological and medical knowledge, and I am aware enough to explain to people that love and care for me about my situation and ordeal.

Do I struggle? Yes, of course, I do. Ordinarily, I am very functional and sound of mind. I can also keep my secret if I'm not. I am healthy and back to whatever you want to call normal. I do not have to blink twice to see that this one year has aged us five years; our faces are drawn and deeply lined. Our eyes are slightly dull still. We move forward and try to live each grateful day as fully as possible.

I am studying and learning about this new version of me!

Thank you again for sticking this out with me, my readers.

WE ARE NOT DONE YET! ARE YOU STILL HERE?

Chapter 12

The Villagers

We have several friends and acquaintances that live in Salinas; some are fishermen by trade and are multi-talented in life's cycles. Over a few years, we have shared beers, many fish-tails, adventures, and storms. Two of our fisherman friends after Maria remembered one of our shared stories about the hurricanes with me working as a housing inspector. They invited me over as a friend to help them and their families understand how they can recuperate and how to evaluate their losses.

To be there and see first-hand the communities and homes of the people I know and care about felt awful. To witness what happened to their homes devastated me.

My heart did a flashback......Hurricane Irwin in Galveston, Texas.

After that disaster, I RETIRED with my heart bleeding. I am an empath!

Today what I saw was homes with a total loss on many accounts. I felt so much love and compassion from them as they shared with everyone they came into contact with. With my experience, I can give them pointers of hope and some advice. I told them that they could take pictures of all the damage and losses.

Due to the greatness of disaster, Maria, there was no possible way to know how long it could take for the housing inspectors to arrive. The USA not only suffered Hurricane Maria but also had their disasters right before our Hurricane to cope with in many states of affairs. There are only so many trained inspectors available. Try to recuperate whatever is possible, clean, sanitize, protect what you can salvage. Think about how important health and safety are. They should be first.

Try drying out your mattress until you can buy another. Then get all the slimy, infected water out of the house. And bleach does wonders to disinfect: be sure to have lots of ventilation during usage and read the label. A picture is worth a thousand words.

I went to visit several family members' homes, only to see so many with total losses and others with the minimal left. Around the corner, a concrete house, all walls and roof standing, but everything inside was ruined. Multiple families now living in one home were a common sight. This is when the Puerto Rican people and families unite because they will share their last pot of food as far as possible, even with a stranger like me — I have been there!

As an inspector, I was just like everyone else: no home, no food, no fuel. There is no electricity to charge the phone so that I can set up a meeting with the families that needed the next inspection. I charge my work computer using my car battery. I slept in my car many nights. The following day I would drive 60 miles from where I could find a hotel or room to sleep in, one that, on regular days, I wouldn't even put my dog in. But I was so exhausted that I didn't give a damn. I was too sleep-deprived to complete the reports by 11:30 pm. I make it to the next house by 6:30 am for inspection, hoping for minimal issues so that they could manage to make it to our appointment. They needed help now. You just do the best you can. I was rationing my water supply, food, snacks, lots of trail mix. As the night is falling fast, I am praying that I do not get stuck on the road without enough fuel. I had access to nothing. I sat in the lines for gas food, just like everyone else.

I saw dead animals along the sidewalk and helped the elderly to get to the Red Cross Center. Many families still had not received any form of communication, and I am their first contact. You are either cut out for this moving emotional part or not. It would take another book to explain how that feels and how I dealt with it. Massive! Though I wouldn't trade this experience, because I have gained valuable wisdom of insight, learning about how humans act and continue to function in the worst conditions. If you ever have an inspector come to your home, please treat them with respect, kindness, and remember to offer them some water!

I think I have a calling to write to you. I feel very

passionate about this. I will make a blog with videos, pictures of the storms, boats in the mangroves. I had no idea this would be my reward for the pain and affliction that WE have been through together.

Let's go homeward bound now to my little island just outside of Puerto Rico. We need to make the same trip that I had explained before. Puerto Rico is still in hardship and a long way from recovery. I pray for us all, as it is the first day of the hurricane season June 2018,, I thought that I was finished writing this story.

There is not a chance on Jan 15, 2019, I'm still writing, and learning how to edit, Along with this challenging task, come more memories to cope with

Chapter 13

Shedding the Old Skin

Today was a wondrous day. I have been waiting over a year for a sign from the Creators of the universe. A couple of years ago, I pledged my word of honor to never ask or beg for neither mercy nor salvation from the possible death of myself and loved ones. If only they would extend the lives of my family this one time in this apparent life and death situation. I have lived up to this promise, but I have felt a loss in my faith because of this. I have felt wounded until a new friend was reading my book and shared her insight with me.

She said to me sweetly, "If one of your children made a solemn promise to you never to ask your forgiveness, help, or mercy, and when they didn't come to you, in their time of desperate need, how would you feel about this?"

I solemnly replied, that I would be ashamed if they felt like they had to live up to such a word of honor that holds them from coming to me, as I have so much love and forgiveness to give. In my eyes, these are only words because I hear the heart and soul. Exactly! My new friend said. "Don't you think the Creator and the universe in which you so much believe in, feel the same way about you?"

They, too, hear the heart and soul.

Don't underestimate the power of the Creator. Prayers can be answered with revelations of inspiration. I see the light once more. Hallelujah.

Chapter 14

More Recovery

I thought my reservoir for tears was dry, but I was reclining in the dentist's chair, getting a tooth pulled should have been a painless procedure. I realize that I have issues. At first, just warm water was running out of my eyes. Maybe you have been there. It is like a faucet stream, and I do not know where the shut-off valve is. The dentist stopped her process, and I broke down sobbing uncontrollably, doubled up in her chair. She asked me if it was painful, and I explained that it is a different kind of pain that I am feeling.

There is a saying that it is good to let the waters run once in a while.

I am waiting for healing waters.

"Maybe we should stop," she says, as she walks away. I start shaking.

After five minutes she returns with genuine concern in her eyes, she knows me; I am not a new patient. She asks me if I am going to be alright. I make eye contact and nod my head. Then she asks me if I am READY?

READY is a trigger word for me, as you might remember. "Yes," I say, sitting upright stiffly, squinting, my eyes tightly closed, opening my mouth bravely and wide.

(READY to begin to live a new life with all the expectations I deserve!)

I am learning about this new version of me! The trauma-drama of Maria will no longer be part of my new identity.

I hope that there are some lessons in this book

you don't have to experience first-hand.

Thanks for having me on-board!! I do not wish to write a sequel. But I do have years and miles of stories to share with you and will continue to do so, writing them under True Stories of the Old Woman and Sea.

PS September 2019 is here, and upon returning to the origin of my source of pain in the mangroves, we are still in Culebra, Puerto Rico, tying up the lines once more for Hurricane Dorian, then on to Salinas for Karen. Yes, we stayed on-board. I feel no nausea or fear. You just have to be prepared for the worst, knowing your boat is ready and hope for the best.

Hubby is 73, and I am 65. We have survived nine major hurricanes on our boats. What can I say, other than my hubby is a real hurricane magnet. The book has been finished for seven months. Though, I still have a lot to learn and a lot more to share. I know most of the time it's not my choice when this level of intensity happens. The beauty is you allowing the experiences, and then growing and learning from them. My dialogue with myself is evidence of how present I am in watching the experience. I will let go of my daily searching for the woman I use to be.

#1 Learn how to tie knots, especially a bowline.

#2 Always have a bailer tied on.

#3 Only use waterproof electronics in the dinghy.

#4 Have a grab bag ready with food and water at all times during a storm.

#5 Make a plan of action, share it with a friend for back-up.

#6 Never take the bottom floor in a hurricane. Move the kayaks, ha-ha

#7 Only rely on a handheld waterproof GPS, fully charged.

#8 Keep faith and hope whenever you are in trouble.

#9 Don't underestimate the power of the Creator of the universe

#10 READY to begin to live a new life with all the expectations you deserver

#11 Long-term use of ibuprofen will give you a painful stomach ulcer, I got a cat scan, and that was the results.

#12 Look in the eyes of adversity and tell yourself that you can make it.

With lots of love,

Allie